To Tommy, grandfather of all Hueys

PHILOMEL BOOKS

A division of Penguin Young Readers Group.

Published by The Penguin Group.

Penguin Group (USA) Inc., 375 Hudson Street, New York, NY 10014, U.S.A.

Penguin Group (Canada), 90 Eglinton Avenue East, Suite 700, Toronto, Ontario M4P 2Y3, Canada (a division of Pearson Penguin Canada Inc.).

Penguin Books Ltd, 80 Strand, London WC2R 0RL, England.

Penguin Ireland, 25 St. Stephen's Green, Dublin 2, Ireland
(a division of Penguin Books Ltd).

Penguin Group (Australia), 250 Camberwell Road, Camberwell, Victoria 3124, Australia (a division of Pearson Australia Group Pty Ltd).

Penguin Books India Pvt Ltd, 11 Community Centre, Panchsheel Park, New Delhi - 110 017, India.

Penguin Group (NZ), 67 Apollo Drive, Rosedale, Auckland 0632, New Zealand (a division of Pearson New Zealand Ltd).

Penguin Books (South Africa) (Pty) Ltd, 24 Sturdee Avenue, Rosebank, Johannesburg 2196, South Africa.

Penguin Books Ltd, Registered Offices: 80 Strand, London WC2R 0RL, England.

Manufactured in Hong Kong

The Hueys were made with pencils and a bit of orange.

Library of Congress Cataloging-in-Publication Data
is available upon request.

ISBN 978-0-399-25767-4

10 9 8 7 6 5 4 3 2 1

The HUEYS in THE NEW SWEATER

OLIVER JEFFERS

PHILOMEL BOOKS
An Imprint of Penguin Group (USA) Inc.

The thing about the Hueys . . .

. . . was that they were all the same.

There were many, many of them . . .

. . . and they
all looked
the same,

thought the
same . . .

and

did

the

same

things . . .

. . . until the day one of them—
Rupert was his name—knitted
a nice new sweater.

He wore it all over the place,
proud as could be.

Not
everyone
agreed with
his taste,
though . . .

In fact, most of the other Hueys
were horrified!

Rupert stood out
like a sore thumb.

Didn't he know that the thing about Hueys was that they were all the same?

Rupert went to Gillespie.

Gillespie thought being different
was interesting.

He decided to knit
himself a nice new
sweater to match.

That way,
he would be
different too!

When the other Hueys saw Gillespie
beside him, they didn't think that
Rupert was so strange anymore.

Being different was catching on . . .

more YARN

. . . and
the others
wanted to
be different
too!

One by one,
new sweaters
started
popping up
everywhere.

Before long, they were all
different, and no one was
the same anymore.

Then Rupert decided
he liked the idea of
wearing a hat.

And that changed everything . . .